# The Care Bears
## and the
# Terrible Twos

**A Random House PICTUREBACK®**

# The Care Bears

by **ALI REICH**

illustrated by
**CAROLYN BRACKEN**

Random House ⌂ New York

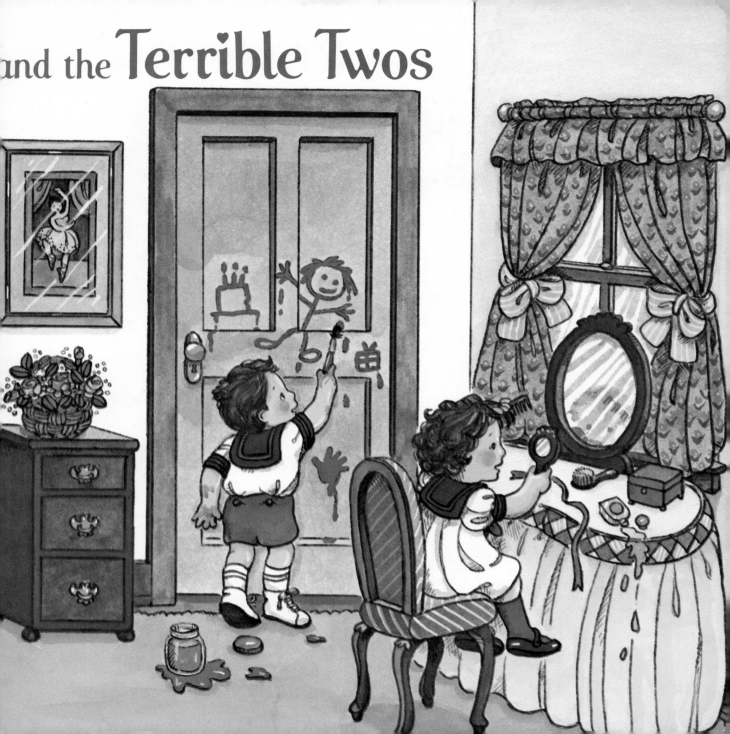

The Care Bears were playing high above the clouds in their magical land, called Care-a-lot.

Down below in the real world, Melinda Higgins was getting ready to start a special day. She hopped out of bed as soon as she woke up and zipped up the new jump suit her grandmother had sent her.

Then she ran downstairs as fast as her sneakers would go.

"Happy birthday!" said her mother and father.

"Happy birthday!" said her sister and brother. They were two-year-old twins.

"A birthday is a very special day," said her mother. "So I fixed your favorite breakfast—pancakes!"

"I want a pancake," said Tess.
"Me too!" said Tommy.
"There are plenty of pancakes for everyone," said Mr. Higgins.

"I want syrup," said Tommy.

"Me too!" said Tess.

"Melinda will pour some for you," said Mrs. Higgins.

"I can do it myself," said Tess.

"Me too!" said Tommy.

Kerplop! The pitcher went flying, and the gooey syrup went drip, drip, drip, all over Melinda.

"You two always spoil everything!" she said. "Now you're even trying to spoil my birthday!"

Up in Care-a-lot, Cheer Bear said, "Uh-oh, there's a girl
named Melinda who needs us."
"It's her birthday, so I'll go," said Birthday Bear.
"I'll come along too," said Grumpy Bear.

So the Care Bears tumbled down, down, down and floated on a little white cloud right over the Higginses' house. Because they are very special Bears, nobody even saw them.

Mr. Higgins was putting Melinda's new jump suit in the washing machine.

Mrs. Higgins was shampooing Melinda's hair. She had to do it two times to get all the syrup out.

The twins were playing with blocks.

"I'll go check on the twins,"
said Mrs. Higgins. "I can't trust
that terrible twosome for long.
I'm glad I can count on you
to dry your hair and get
dressed."

So Melinda got dressed. She packed her toothbrush, a sweater, and her doll in a paper bag and wrote a note. It said:

Dear Mom and Dad, I can't stand those terrible twos any longer. I'm leaving! Love, Melinda

After Mr. Higgins left for work, Mrs. Higgins began to mix a cake in the kitchen.

The twins were playing in the living room.

"I'm having a shampoo like Melinda," said Tess. She poured ketchup all over her head.

"Me too," said Tommy.

Everyone was so busy
that no one saw Melinda
and the Care Bears leave.

"Where will you live?"
asked Birthday Bear.

"I don't quite know,"
answered Melinda.

"Let's go to your tree
house and think about it,"
said Cheer Bear.

So Melinda climbed up into the tree house. The Care Bears
went with her. Melinda thought and thought.
"I know! I could join the circus!"

"You could swing on the trapeze!" said Cheer Bear.

"You could ride an elephant!" said Birthday Bear.

"Maybe I could even be the tiger trainer!" said Melinda.

"But you're not old enough to join the circus,"
said Grumpy Bear.

"I could live at Grandma's house."

"It's much too far to walk," said Grumpy Bear.

"Maybe I could live where Daddy works."

"That's not such a good idea," said Grumpy Bear.
"We'd better think some more."

Melinda's jump suit danced in the gentle breeze.
Soon they all smelled something wonderful.
"Hmmm! It's Melinda's cake," said Birthday Bear.
"Come home, Melinda," cried Tommy. "I'll be good."
"Me too," said Tess. "Come home, Melinda. Come home!"

asked the Care

"Not for a while," sa___ ____mpy ____.

"I think they'll try," said Cheer Bear.

"In a couple of months they'll have their own birthday," said Birthday Bear. "They won't be the terrible twos then."

"Look!" said Cheer Bear. "Those boys and girls are going right to your house!"

"They'll be very disappointed if you're not there!" said Grumpy Bear.

"I think the best place for you to go is home," said Cheer Bear.

"Me too," said Melinda.

"Surprise! Happy birthday!" said Melinda's friends.

"I love Melinda!" said Tess.

"Me too!" said Tommy.

Even though she knew the twins were still terrible, Melinda was very happy.

The twins didn't spill anything at her party. It *was* a special day.